Shadow
and Johnny

Enid Blyton

Illustrated by Rowan Clifford

CARNIVAL

Shadow the sheepdog was growing up. He was
now six months old and it was time for him to
begin his training.

His master, Johnny, called Shadow to him.

"Shadow, you must learn some lessons now,"
said Johnny to his puppy. "Jessie, your mother,
has taught you quite a lot of things, but I must
teach you some too. You must learn to know my
whistle and come at once when you are called,
no matter WHAT you are doing. That's the
first lesson. I'll teach you today."

Shadow listened, his tail wagging like a windmill. What an easy lesson! He already knew Johnny's whistle by heart. He knew his shout too. There was no voice in the world like Johnny's, Shadow was sure. He loved Johnny's smell too. Even Johnny's footsteps smelt of Johnny. Sometimes Shadow would find some in the yard and would spend a lovely minute following up the smell of the footprints until he came to Johnny himself.

"You have a sharp nose, Shadow," Johnny said to him. "That's good. One day it may be useful to you, if a sheep is lost."

Johnny took Shadow out into the fields. Shadow loved the fields because of the exciting smells everywhere. He ran about, his nose to the ground, smelling rat, mouse, hedgehog, rabbit, hare, and fox. He put his head down a rabbit-hole and a smell of rabbit came up.

Shadow went quite mad. He began to sniff and scrape, his nose well down the hole. Johnny smiled a little and went on down the field, leaving Shadow behind. Now the puppy was to get his first lesson!

When he was at the end of the field, Johnny stopped. Shadow was still scraping at the rabbit-hole. Johnny whistled. "Pheeeeeeeeee!"

Shadow heard the whistle – but how could he leave this exciting rabbit-smell? Why, he might get to the rabbit in half a minute! He took no notice of Johnny's whistle and went on sniffing and scrabbling.

"PHHHHHHHHHEEEEEEEEE!" The whistle came again, much louder. Shadow took his head out of the hole. He saw Johnny waiting for him. He wondered if he should go. No – Johnny could wait a minute till he got that rabbit! And into the hole went his eager puppy-head again.

Then Johnny shouted loudly: "Shadow! Shadow! Come here!"

But still Shadow didn't come. He felt he couldn't leave such a wonderful rabbit-smell.

And then Johnny walked all the way back till he came to the puppy. Shadow felt Johnny's hand pull on his collar. He took his head out of the hole and looked up in astonishment at Johnny. Johnny was angry! Oh, what a very dreadful thing!

"Shadow! You heard me whistle, Pheeee, and you didn't come. You heard me call you loudly, and you didn't come. You are a bad dog."

Poor Shadow! His tail was lost between his legs, his ears drooped, he couldn't look at Johnny. He crept after him, whining softly, the most unhappy and ashamed dog in all the world. Never, never would he put a rabbit-hole before his master again.

When they came to another rabbit-hole Johnny stopped. "Rabbits!" he said. "Rabbits! Go in and fetch them then."

Shadow at once went to scrape and sniff at the hole, and in a trice Johnny ran down the field. He turned and whistled. He must see if the puppy had learnt his first lesson! "PHEEEEE!" The whistle went loud and clear over the field.

And this time Shadow took his head out of the hole at once, and tore off to Johnny as fast as his legs could carry him! He wasn't going to be scolded again!

"Good dog, Shadow, good dog!" said Johnny
and he patted the puppy proudly. "It didn't
take you long to learn that lesson, did it! I don't
believe you'll need teaching that one again."

He certainly didn't. At the first sound of
Johnny's shrill whistle, Shadow always bounded
off to him at once. Then he was taught his next
lesson – to walk exactly at Johnny's heels when
he went into the town, or for walks.

"You see, Shadow, a good-mannered dog must walk just behind his master, so as not to get in his way," said Johnny. "And he must always be at heel in case he is wanted. So when I say, 'Heel!' to you, you must walk just there – that's it – your nose almost touching my shoe. When I take your lead off and say 'Run, Shadow,' you may leave my heels and go bounding about for a run."

Shadow listened hard. He didn't much like walking just behind Johnny in the town. There were so many things to see and smell there. He wanted to stop and sniff at everything. He wanted to run up to the dogs he met and tell them about Johnny.

But Johnny kept Shadow on his lead. If Shadow's nose came too far in front instead of keeping to heel, Johnny would give a sharp jerk on the lead. So he soon learnt that Johnny meant what he said. "Heel" meant walking just behind Johnny and nothing else – he mustn't pull on his lead and he mustn't loiter. He was a clever little dog, so it didn't take him more than two days to learn that lesson.

"Now you must teach him to be 'On guard',
Johnny," said his father. "That is important for
a sheepdog."

So Shadow was taught what "On guard"
meant. It was not so easy to learn that! Johnny
took him into a field and put his jacket down on
the grass. He made Shadow sit on it.

"On guard!" he said. "On guard, Shadow!
You mustn't leave my jacket till I come back or
whistle to you. You are guarding it."

"Woof," said Shadow happily. He liked
sitting on anything belonging to Johnny.

Johnny began to walk away. At once Shadow bounded after him, leaving the jacket. Johnny swung round and looked down at him sternly.

"Didn't I tell you to guard it!" he cried. "Bad dog! Go back. On guard, I tell you, on guard."

He took Shadow back to his jacket and made him sit on it again. Shadow's tail drooped. He didn't want to stay with a jacket. He wanted to go with Johnny.

Johnny set off again. Shadow waited till he had turned a corner and then bounded after him. But no, that was not the right thing to do at all! Johnny spoke angrily to him, and Shadow was miserable. Perhaps the jacket was very important, he thought.

"Have I got to take you all the way back again!" cried Johnny. "Bad dog. I put you on guard, on guard, on guard!"

Shadow understood. He had to go back and stay with that silly jacket till further orders. Well – he didn't understand *why* – but all the same he knew he must obey. So back he went of his own accord, and lay down on the jacket, his chin on his two front paws.

Johnny went into the next field and waited a few minutes. He peeped through the hedge and saw that Shadow was really on guard this time. "What a good little fellow he is!" thought the boy proudly. "Now I'll go back and give him a biscuit for a reward. It was hard for him to learn that lesson."

He went back. Shadow saw him coming and stood up joyfully, his tail wagging wildly. But he didn't leave the jacket. No – he knew that he was meant to stay with it, on guard until Johnny came right up to him.

And then it was worth being taught the lesson
when Johnny fed him with a delicious biscuit
and patted him and told him he was the most
marvellous dog in the world! Shadow rolled over
on his back, put all his fat legs into the air and
yelped for joy.

Johnny put on his jacket. "Another lesson
learnt!" he said. "Good dog!"

Shadow learnt to let Johnny take away his
bone from him, without growling or snapping.
He learnt to track Johnny wherever he was, even
when he was a mile or two away. That was
really clever. Johnny would shut him up in a
kennel, and go off for a walk. Then, half an hour
later a farm-hand would let him out and say,
"Now find Johnny! Go find Johnny, Shadow!
Where's Johnny!"

And Shadow would put his nose to the ground and run wildly about until he found a fresh footstep of Johnny's. Then off he would go, like an arrow from a bow, smelling Johnny's track without a mistake. Over field and hedge, ditch and stream, he would run – and at last would find Johnny, hidden up a tree, or in the heather!

"Good dog! You've only taken ten minutes this time!" cried Johnny. "Do you like your lessons, Shadow? You learn them quickly enough! Soon you must go off with the other sheepdogs and learn how to round up the sheep. I guess you'll be the cleverest sheepdog Daddy's ever had on the farm. You will try hard, won't you, Shadow?"

"Woof," said Shadow, licking his master's hand over and over again. He was excited to hear he was to go with the big dogs – he would show them how clever he would be with the sheep!